I0624236

The
Libation Bearers

The
Libation Bearers
Aeschylus

MINT EDITIONS

The Libation Bearers was first published in 458 BC.

This edition published by Mint Editions 2020.

ISBN 9781513270319 | E-ISBN 9781513275314

Published by Mint Editions®

 MINT
EDITIONS
minteditionbooks.com

Publishing Director: Jennifer Newens
Design & Production: Rachel Lopez Metzger
Translated by: E.D.A. MORSHEAD
Project Manager: Micaela Clark
Typesetting: Westchester Publishing Services

Dramatis Personae

ORESTES
CHORUS OF CAPTIVE WOMEN
ELECTRA
A NURSE
CLYTEMNESTRA
AEGISTHUS
AN ATTENDANT
PYLADES

The Scene is the Tomb of Agamemnon at Mycenae; afterwards, the Palace of Atreus, hard by the Tomb.

ORESTES: Lord of the shades and patron of the realm
That erst my father swayed, list now my prayer,
Hermes, and save me with thine aiding arm,
Me who from banishment returning stand
On this my country; lo, my foot is set
On this grave-mound, and herald-like, as thou,
Once and again, I bid my father hear.
And these twin locks, from mine head shorn, I bring,
And one to Inachus the river-god,
My young life's nurturer, I dedicate,
And one in sign of mourning unfulfilled
I lay, though late, on this my father's grave.
For O my father, not beside thy corse
Stood I to wail thy death, nor was my hand
Stretched out to bear thee forth to burial.

What sight is yonder? what this woman-throng
Hitherward coming, by their sable garb
Made manifest as mourners? What hath chanced?
Doth some new sorrow hap within the home?
Or rightly may I deem that they draw near
Bearing libations, such as soothe the ire
Of dead men angered, to my father's grave?
Nay, such they are indeed; for I descry
Electra mine own sister pacing hither,
In moody grief conspicuous. Grant, O Zeus,
Grant me my father's murder to avenge—
Be thou my willing champion!
                                                    Pylades,
Pass we aside, till rightly I discern
Wherefore these women throng in suppliance.

(*Exeunt Pylades and Orestes; enter the Chorus bearing vessels for libation; Electra follows them; they pace slowly towards the tomb of Agamemnon*)

CHORUS: Forth from the royal halls by high command
        I bear libations for the dead.
Rings on my smitten breast my smiting hand,
        And all my cheek is rent and red,
Fresh-furrowed by my nails, and all my soul

This many a day doth feed on cries of dole.
　　And trailing tatters of my vest,
In looped and windowed raggedness forlorn,
　　Hang rent around my breast,
Even as I, by blows of Fate most stern
　　Saddened and torn.

　　Oracular thro' visions, ghastly clear,
Bearing a blast of wrath from realms below,
And stiffening each rising hair with dread,
　　Came out of dream-land Fear,
　　And, loud and awful, bade
The shriek ring out at midnight's witching hour,
　　And brooded, stern with woe,
Above the inner house, the woman's bower.
And seers inspired did read the dream on oath,
　　Chanting aloud *In realms below*
　　　　The dead are wroth;
Against their slayers yet their ire doth glow.

Therefore to bear this gift of graceless worth—
　　O Earth, my nursing mother!—
The woman god-accurs'd doth send me forth
　　Lest one crime bring another.
Ill is the very word to speak, for none
　　　　Can ransom or atone
For blood once shed and darkening the plain.
　　　　O hearth of woe and bane,
　　　　O state that low doth lie!
Sunless, accursed of men, the shadows brood
　　Above the home of murdered majesty.

Rumour of might, unquestioned, unsubdued,
Pervading ears and soul of lesser men,
　　　　Is silent now and dead.
　　　　Yet rules a viler dread;
　　For bliss and power, however won,
As gods, and more than gods, dazzle our mortal ken.

Justice doth mark, with scales that swiftly sway,
    Some that are yet in light;
    Others in interspace of day and night,
       Till Fate arouse them, stay;
And some are lapped in night, where all things are undone.

On the life-giving lap of Earth
    Blood hath flowed forth;
And now, the seed of vengeance, clots the plain—
    Unmelting, uneffaced the stain.
And Atè tarries long, but at the last
       The sinner's heart is cast
Into pervading, waxing pangs of pain.

    Lo, when man's force doth ope
The virgin doors, there is nor cure nor hope
    For what is lost,—even so, I deem,
Though in one channel ran Earth's every stream,
    Laving the hand defiled from murder's stain,
       It were vain.

And upon me—ah me!—the gods have laid
    The woe that wrapped round Troy,
What time they led down from home and kin
       Unto a slave's employ—
    The doom to bow the head
    And watch our master's will
       Work deeds of good and ill—
To see the headlong sway of force and sin,
    And hold restrained the spirit's bitter hate,
    Wailing the monarch's fruitless fate,
  Hiding my face within my robe, and fain
Of tears, and chilled with frost of hidden pain.

ELECTRA: Hand maidens, orderers of the palace-halls,
    Since at my side ye come, a suppliant train,
    Companions of this offering, counsel me
    As best befits the time: for I, who pour
    Upon the grave these streams funereal,

With what fair word can I invoke my sire?
Shall I aver, *Behold, I bear these gifts*
From well-beloved wife unto her well-beloved lord,
When 'tis from her, my mother, that they come?
I dare not say it: of all words I fail
Wherewith to consecrate unto my sire
These sacrificial honours on his grave.
Or shall I speak this word, as mortals use—
Give back, to those who send these coronals
Full recompense—of ills for acts malign?
Or shall I pour this draught for Earth to drink,
Sans word or reverence, as my sire was slain,
And homeward pass with unreverted eyes,
Casting the bowl away, as one who flings
The household cleansings to the common road?
Be art and part, O friends, in this my doubt,
Even as ye are in that one common hate
Whereby we live attended: fear ye not
The wrath of any man, nor hide your word
Within your breast: the day of death and doom
Awaits alike the freeman and the slave.
Speak, then, if aught thou know'st to aid us more.
CHORUS: Thou biddest; I will speak my soul's thought out,
Revering as a shrine thy father's grave.
ELECTRA: Say then thy say, as thou his tomb reverest.
CHORUS: Speak solemn words to them that love, and pour.
ELECTRA: And of his kin whom dare I name as kind?
CHORUS: Thyself; and next, whoe'er Aegisthus scorns.
ELECTRA: Then 'tis myself and thou, my prayer must name.
CHORUS: Whoe'er they be, 'tis thine to know and name them.
ELECTRA: Is there no other we may claim as ours?
CHORUS: Think of Orestes, though far-off he be.
ELECTRA: Right well in this too hast thou schooled my thought.
CHORUS: Mindfully, next, on those who shed the blood—
ELECTRA: Pray on them what? expound, instruct my doubt.
CHORUS: This; *Upon them some god or mortal come—*
ELECTRA: As judge or as avenger? speak thy thought.
CHORUS: Pray in set terms, *Who shall the slayer slay.*

ELECTRA: Beseemeth it to ask such boon of heaven?
CHORUS: How not, to wreak a wrong upon a foe?
ELECTRA: O mighty Hermes, warder of the shades,
  Herald of upper and of under world,
  Proclaim and usher down my prayer's appeal
  Unto the gods below, that they with eyes
  Watchful behold these halls, my sire's of old—
  And unto Earth, the mother of all things,
  And foster-nurse, and womb that takes their seed.

  Lo, I that pour these draughts for men now dead,
  Call on my father, who yet holds in ruth
  Me and mine own Orestes, *Father, speak—*
  How shall thy children rule thine halls again?
  Homeless we are and sold; and she who sold
  Is she who bore us; and the price she took
  Is he who joined with her to work thy death,
  Aegisthus, her new lord. Behold me here
  Brought down to slave's estate, and far away
  Wanders Orestes, banished from the wealth
  That once was thine, the profit of thy care,
  Whereon these revel in a shameful joy.
  Father, my prayer is said; 'tis thine to hear—
  Grant that some fair fate bring Orestes home,
  And unto me grant these—a purer soul
  Than is my mother's, a more stainless hand.

  These be my prayers for us; for thee, O sire,
  I cry that one may come to smite thy foes,
  And that the slayers may in turn be slain.
  Cursed is their prayer, and thus I bar its path,
  Praying mine own, a counter-curse on them.
  And thou, send up to us the righteous boon
  For which we pray: thine aids be heaven and earth,
  And justice guide the right to victory,
(*To the Chorus*)
  Thus have I prayed, and thus I shed these streams,
  And follow ye the wont, and as with flowers

Crown ye with many a tear and cry the dirge,
Your lips ring out above the dead man's grave.
(*She pours the libations*)
CHORUS: Woe, woe, woe!
Let the teardrop fall, plashing on the ground
Where our lord lies low:
Fall and cleanse away the cursed libation's stain,
Shed on this grave-mound,
Fenced wherein together, gifts of good or bane
From the dead are found.
Lord of Argos, hearken!
Though around thee darken
Mist of death and hell, arise and hear!
Hearken and awaken to our cry of woe!
Who with might of spear
Shall our home deliver?
Who like Ares bend until it quiver,
Bend the northern bow?
Who with hand upon the hilt himself will thrust with glaive,
Thrust and slay and save?
ELECTRA: Lo! the earth drinks them, to my sire they pass—
Learn ye with me of this thing new and strange.
CHORUS: Speak thou; my breast doth palpitate with fear.
ELECTRA: I see upon the tomb a curl new shorn.
CHORUS: Shorn from what man or what deep-girded maid?
ELECTRA: That may he guess who will; the sign is plain.
CHORUS: Let me learn this of thee; let youth prompt age.
ELECTRA: None is there here but I, to clip such gift.
CHORUS: For they who thus should mourn him hate him sore.
ELECTRA: And lo! in truth the hair exceeding like—
CHORUS: Like to what locks and whose? instruct me that.
ELECTRA: Like unto those my father's children wear.
CHORUS: Then is this lock Orestes' secret gift?
ELECTRA: Most like it is unto the curls he wore,
CHORUS: Yet how dared he to come unto his home?
ELECTRA: He hath but sent it, clipt to mourn his sire.
CHORUS: It is a sorrow grievous as his death,
That he should live yet never dare return.
ELECTRA: Yea, and my heart o'erflows with gall of grief,

And I am pierced as with a cleaving dart;
Like to the first drops after drought, my tears
Fall down at will, a bitter bursting tide,
As on this lock I gaze; I cannot deem
That any Argive save Orestes' self
Was ever lord thereof; nor, well I wot,
Hath she, the murd'ress, shorn and laid this lock
To mourn him whom she slew—my mother she,
Bearing no mother's heart, but to her race
A loathing spirit, loathed itself of heaven!
Yet to affirm, as utterly made sure,
That this adornment cometh of the hand
Of mine Orestes, brother of my soul,
I may not venture, yet hope flatters fair!
Ah well-a-day, that this dumb hair had voice
To glad mine ears, as might a messenger,
Bidding me sway no more 'twixt fear and hope,
Clearly commanding, *Cast me hence away,*
Clipped was I from some head thou lovest not;
Or, *I am kin to thee, and here, as thou,*
I come to weep and deck our father's grave.
Aid me, ye gods! for well indeed ye know
How in the gale and counter-gale of doubt,
Like to the seaman's bark, we whirl and stray.
But, if God will our life, how strong shall spring,
From seed how small, the new tree of our home!—
Lo ye, a second sign—these footsteps, look,—
Like to my own, a corresponsive print;
And look, another footmark,—this his own,
And that the foot of one who walked with him.
Mark, how the heel and tendons' print combine,
Measured exact, with mine coincident!
Alas! for doubt and anguish rack my mind.
ORESTES: (*approaching suddenly*) Pray thou, in gratitude for prayers
    fulfilled, *Fair fall the rest of what I ask of heaven.*
ELECTRA: Wherefore? what win I from the gods by prayer?
ORESTES: This, that thine eyes behold thy heart's desire.
ELECTRA: On whom of mortals know'st thou that I call?
ORESTES: I know thy yearning for Orestes deep.

ELECTRA: Say then, wherein event hath crowned
    my prayer?
ORESTES: I, I am he; seek not one more akin.
ELECTRA: Some fraud, O stranger, weavest thou for me?
ORESTES: Against myself I weave it, if I weave.
ELECTRA: Ah, thou hast mind to mock me in my woe!
ORESTES: 'Tis at mine own I mock then, mocking thine.
ELECTRA: Speak I with thee then as Orestes' self?
ORESTES: My very face thou see'st and know'st me not,
    And yet but now, when thou didst see the lock
    Shorn for my father's grave, and when thy quest
    Was eager on the footprints I had made,
    Even I, thy brother, shaped and sized as thou,
    Fluttered thy spirit, as at sight of me!
    Lay now this ringlet whence 'twas shorn, and judge,
    And look upon this robe, thine own hands' work,
    The shuttle-prints, the creature wrought thereon—
    Refrain thyself, nor prudence lose in joy,
    For well I wot, our kin are less than kind.
ELECTRA: O thou that art unto our father's home
    Love, grief and hope, for thee the tears ran down,
    For thee, the son, the saviour that should be;
    Trust thou thine arm and win thy father's halls!
    O aspect sweet of fourfold love to me,
    Whom upon thee the heart's constraint bids call
    As on my father, and the claim of love
    From me unto my mother turns to thee,
    For she is very hate; to thee too turns
    What of my heart went out to her who died
    A ruthless death upon the altar-stone;
    And for myself I love thee—thee that wast
    A brother leal, sole stay of love to me.
    Now by thy side be strength and right, and Zeus
    Saviour almighty, stand to aid the twain!
ORESTES: Zeus, Zeus! look down on our estate and us,
    The orphaned brood of him, our eagle-sire,
    Whom to his death a fearful serpent brought
    Enwinding him in coils; and we, bereft
    And foodless, sink with famine, all too weak

To bear unto the eyrie, as he bore,
Such quarry as he slew. Lo! I and she,
Electra, stand before thee, fatherless,
And each alike cast out and homeless made.

ELECTRA: And if thou leave to death the brood of him
Whose altar blazed for thee, whose reverence
Was thine, all thine,—whence, in the after years,
Shall any hand like his adorn thy shrine
With sacrifice of flesh? the eaglets slain,
Thou wouldst not have a messenger to bear
Thine omens, once so clear, to mortal men;
So, if this kingly stock be withered all,
None on high festivals will fend thy shrine
Stoop thou to raise us! strong the race shall show,
Though puny now it seem, and fallen low.

CHORUS: O children, saviours of your father's home,
Beware ye of your words, lest one should hear
And bear them, for the tongue hath lust to tell,
Unto our masters—whom God grant to me
In pitchy reek of fun'ral flame to see!

ORESTES: Nay, mighty is Apollo's oracle
And shall not fail me, whom it bade to pass
Thro' all this peril; clear the voice rang out
With many warnings, sternly threatening
To my hot heart the wintry chill of pain,
Unless upon the slayers of my sire
I pressed for vengeance: this the god's command—
That I, in ire for home and wealth despoiled,
Should with a craft like theirs the slayers slay:
Else with my very life I should atone
This deed undone, in many a ghastly wise
For he proclaimed unto the ears of men
That offerings, poured to angry power of death,
Exude again, unless their will be done,
As grim disease on those that poured them forth—
As leprous ulcers mounting on the flesh
And with fell fangs corroding what of old
Wore natural form; and on the brow arise
White poisoned hairs, the crown of this disease.

He spake moreover of assailing fiends
Empowered to quit on me my father's blood,
Wreaking their wrath on me, what time in night
Beneath shut lids the spirit's eye sees clear.
The dart that flies in darkness, sped from hell
By spirits of the murdered dead who call
Unto their kin for vengeance, formless fear,
The night-tide's visitant, and madness' curse
Should drive and rack me; and my tortured frame
Should be chased forth from man's community
As with the brazen scorpions of the scourge.
For me and such as me no lustral bowl
Should stand, no spilth of wine be poured to God
For me, and wrath unseen of my dead sire
Should drive me from the shrine; no man should dare
To take me to his hearth, nor dwell with me:
Slow, friendless, cursed of all should be mine end,
And pitiless horror wind me for the grave,
This spake the god—this dare I disobey?
Yea, though I dared, the deed must yet be done;
For to that end diverse desires combine,—
The god's behest, deep grief for him who died,
And last, the grievous blank of wealth despoiled—
All these weigh on me, urge that Argive men,
Minions of valour, who with soul of fire
Did make of fencèd Troy a ruinous heap,
Be not left slaves to two and each a woman!
For he, the man, wears woman's heart; if not
Soon shall he know, confronted by a man.

(Orestes, Electra, and the Chorus gather round the tomb of Agamemnon for the invocation which follows)

CHORUS: Mighty Fates, on you we call!
   Bid the will of Zeus ordain
   Power to those, to whom again
   Justice turns with hand and aid!
   Grievous was the prayer one made—
   Grievous let the answer fall!
   Where the mighty doom is set,
   Justice claims aloud her debt

Who in blood hath dipped the steel,
Deep in blood her meed shall feel!
List an immemorial word—
Whosoe'er shall take the sword
Shall perish by the sword.

ORESTES: Father, unblest in death, O father mine!
What breath of word or deed
Can I waft on thee from this far confine
Unto thy lowly bed,—
Waft upon thee, in midst of darkness lying,
Hope's counter-gleam of fire?
Yet the loud dirge of praise brings grace undying
Unto each parted sire.

CHORUS: O child, the spirit of the dead,
Altho' upon his flesh have fed
The grim teeth of the flame,
Is quelled not; after many days
The sting of wrath his soul shall raise,
A vengeance to reclaim!
To the dead rings loud our cry—
Plain the living's treachery—
Swelling, shrilling, urged on high,
The vengeful dirge, for parents slain,
Shall strive and shall attain.

ELECTRA: Hear me too, even me, O father, hear!
Not by one child alone these groans, these tears are shed
Upon thy sepulchre.
Each, each, where thou art lowly laid,
Stands, a suppliant, homeless made:
Ah, and all is full of ill,
Comfort is there none to say!
Strive and wrestle as we may,
Still stands doom invincible.

CHORUS: Nay, if so he will, the god
Still our tears to joy can turn
He can bid a triumph-ode
Drown the dirge beside this urn;
He to kingly halls can greet
The child restored, the homeward-guided feet.

ORESTES: Ah my father! hadst thou lain
    Under Ilion's wall,
  By some Lycian spearman slain,
    Thou hadst left in this thine hall
  Honour; thou hadst wrought for us
  Fame and life most glorious.
    Over-seas if thou had'st died,
  Heavily had stood thy tomb,
    Heaped on high; but, quenched in pride,
  Grief were light unto thy home.
CHORUS: Loved and honoured hadst thou lain
    By the dead that nobly fell,
  In the under-world again,
    Where are throned the kings of hell,
    Full of sway adorable
  Thou hadst stood at their right hand—
  Thou that wert, in mortal land,
    By Fate's ordinance and law,
  King of kings who bear the crown
    And the staff, to which in awe
  Mortal men bow down.
ELECTRA: Nay O father, I were fain
  Other fate had fallen on thee.
    Ill it were if thou hadst lain
    One among the common slain,
    Fallen by Scamander's side—
  Those who slew thee there should be!
  Then, untouched by slavery,
    We had heard as from afar
  Deaths of those who should have died
    'Mid the chance of war.
CHORUS: O child, forbear! things all too high thou
  sayest.
    Easy, but vain, thy cry!
  A boon above all gold is that thou prayest,
    An unreached destiny,
  As of the blessèd land that far aloof
    Beyond the north wind lies;

Yet doth your double prayer ring loud reproof;
    A double scourge of sighs
Awakes the dead; th' avengers rise, though late;
    Blood stains the guilty pride
Of the accursed who rule on earth, and Fate
    Stands on the children's side.

ELECTRA: That hath sped thro' mine ear, like a shaft from a bow!
  Zeus, Zeus! it is thou who dost send from below
  A doom on the desperate doer—ere long
  On a mother a father shall visit his wrong.

CHORUS: Be it mine to upraise thro' the reek of the pyre
  The chant of delight, while the funeral fire
    Devoureth the corpse of a man that is slain
      And a woman laid low!
  For who bids me conceal it! out-rending control,
  Blows ever stern blast of hate thro' my soul,
    And before me a vision of wrath and of bane
      Flits and waves to and fro.

ORESTES: Zeus, thou alone to us art parent now.
    Smite with a rending blow
  Upon their heads, and bid the land be well:
  Set right where wrong hath stood; and thou give ear,
    O Earth, unto my prayer—
  Yea, hear O mother Earth, and monarchy of hell!

CHORUS: Nay, the law is sternly set—
    Blood-drops shed upon the ground
  Plead for other bloodshed yet;
    Loud the call of death doth sound,
  Calling guilt of olden time,
  A Fury, crowning crime with crime.

ELECTRA: Where, where are ye, avenging powers,
    Puissant Furies of the slain?
    Behold the relics of the race
    Of Atreus, thrust from pride of place!
  O Zeus, what home henceforth is ours,
    What refuge to attain?

CHORUS: Lo, at your wail my heart throbs, wildly stirred;
    Now am I lorn with sadness,

Darkened in all my soul, to hear your sorrow's word.
    Anon to hope, the seat of strength, I rise,—
    She, thrusting grief away, lifts up mine eyes
        To the new dawn of gladness.
ORESTES: Skills it to tell of aught save wrong on wrong,
    Wrought by our mother's deed?
Though now she fawn for pardon, sternly strong
    Standeth our wrath, and will nor hear nor heed;
Her children's soul is wolfish, born from hers,
    And softens not by prayers.
CHORUS: I dealt upon my breast the blow
    That Asian mourning women know;
Wails from my breast the fun'ral cry,
        The Cissian weeping melody;
Stretched rendingly forth, to tatter and tear,
My clenched hands wander, here and there,
        From head to breast; distraught with blows
            Throb dizzily my brows.
ELECTRA: Aweless in hate, O mother, sternly brave!
        As in a foeman's grave
    Thou laid'st in earth a king, but to the bier
        No citizen drew near,—
    Thy husband, thine, yet for his obsequies,
        Thou bad'st no wail arise!
ORESTES: Alas the shameful burial thou dost speak!
    Yet I the vengeance of his shame will wreak—
        That do the gods command!
        That shall achieve mine hand!
    Grant me to thrust her life away, and I
            Will dare to die!
CHORUS: List thou the deed! Hewn down and foully torn,
        He to the tomb was borne;
    Yea, by her hand, the deed who wrought,
    With like dishonour to the grave was brought,
    And by her hand she strove, with strong desire,
    Thy life to crush, O child, by murder of thy sire:
        Bethink thee, hearing, of the shame, the pain
            Wherewith that sire was slain!

ELECTRA: Yea, such was the doom of my sire; well-a-day,
  I was thrust from his side,—
As a dog from the chamber they thrust me away,
And in place of my laughter rose sobbing and tears,
    As in darkness I lay.
O father, if this word can pass to thine ears,
  To thy soul let it reach and abide!
CHORUS: Let it pass, let it pierce, through the sense of
  thine ear,
    To thy soul, where in silence it waiteth the hour!
The past is accomplished; but rouse thee to hear
What the future prepareth; awake and appear,
    Our champion, in wrath and in power!
ORESTES: O father, to thy loved ones come in aid.
ELECTRA: With tears I call on thee.
CHORUS: Listen and rise to light!
  Be thou with us, be thou against the foe!
  Swiftly this cry arises—even so
    Pray we, the loyal band, as we have prayed!
ORESTES: Let their might meet with mine, and their right with my
  right.
ELECTRA: O ye Gods, it is yours to decree.
CHORUS: Ye call unto the dead; I quake to hear.
  Fate is ordained of old, and shall fulfil your prayer.
ELECTRA: Alas, the inborn curse that haunts our home,
    Of Atè's bloodstained scourge the tuneless sound!
  Alas, the deep insufferable doom,
    The stanchless wound!
ORESTES: It shall be stanched, the task is ours,—
    Not by a stranger's, but by kindred hand,
  Shall be chased forth the blood-fiend of our land.
    Be this our spoken spell, to call Earth's nether powers!
CHORUS: Lords of a dark eternity,
  To you has come the children's cry,
  Send up from hell, fulfil your aid
    To them who prayed.
ORESTES: O father, murdered in unkingly wise,
  Fulfil my prayer, grant me thine halls to sway.

ELECTRA: To me too, grant this boon—dark death to deal
    Unto Aegisthus, and to 'scape my doom.
ORESTES: So shall the rightful feasts that mortals pay
    Be set for thee; else, not for thee shall rise
    The scented reek of altars fed with flesh,
    But thou shall lie dishonoured: hear thou me!
ELECTRA: I too, from my full heritage restored,
    Will pour the lustral streams, what time I pass
    Forth as a bride from these paternal halls,
    And honour first, beyond all graves, thy tomb.
ORESTES: Earth, send my sire to fend me in the fight!
ELECTRA: Give fair-faced fortune, O Persephone!
ORESTES: Bethink thee, father, in the laver slain—
ELECTRA: Bethink thee of the net they handselled for thee!
ORESTES: Bonds not of brass ensnared thee, father mine.
ELECTRA: Yea, the ill craft of an enfolding robe.
ORESTES: By this our bitter speech arise, O sire!
ELECTRA: Raise thou thine head at love's last, dearest call!
ORESTES: Yea, speed forth Right to aid thy kinsmen's cause;
    Grip for grip, let them grasp the foe, if thou
    Willest in triumph to forget thy fall.
ELECTRA: Hear me, O father, once again hear me.
    Lo! at thy tomb, two fledglings of thy brood—
    A man-child and a maid; hold them in ruth,
    Nor wipe them out, the last of Pelops' line.
    For while they live, thou livest from the dead;
    Children are memory's voices, and preserve
    The dead from wholly dying: as a net
    Is ever by the buoyant corks upheld,
    Which save the flex-mesh, in the depth submerged.
    Listen, this wail of ours doth rise for thee,
    And as thou heedest it thyself art saved.
CHORUS: In sooth, a blameless prayer ye spake at length—
    The tomb's requital for its dirge denied:
    Now, for the rest, as thou art fixed to do,
    Take fortune by the hand and work thy will.
ORESTES: The doom is set; and yet I fain would ask—
    Not swerving from the course of my resolve,—
    Wherefore she sent these offerings, and why

She softens all too late her cureless deed?
An idle boon it was, to send them here
Unto the dead who recks not of such gifts.
I cannot guess her thought, but well I ween
Such gifts are skilless to atone such crime.
Be blood once spilled, an idle strife he strives
Who seeks with other wealth or wine outpoured
To atone the deed. So stands the word, nor fails.
Yet would I know her thought; speak, if thou knowest.

CHORUS: I know it, son; for at her side I stood.
'Twas the night-wandering terror of a dream
That flung her shivering from her couch, and bade her—
Her, the accursed of God—these offerings send.

ORESTES: Heard ye the dream, to tell it forth aright?

CHORUS: Yea, from herself; her womb a serpent bare.

ORESTES: What then the sum and issue of the tale?

CHORUS: Even as a swaddled child, she lull'd the thing.

ORESTES: What suckling craved the creature, born full-fanged?

CHORUS: Yet in her dreams she proffered it the breast.

ORESTES: How? did the hateful thing not bite her teat?

CHORUS: Yea, and sucked forth a blood-gout in the milk.

ORESTES: Not vain this dream—it bodes a man's revenge.

CHORUS: Then out of sleep she started with a cry,
And thro' the palace for their mistress' aid
Full many lamps, that erst lay blind with night,
Flared into light; then, even as mourners use,
She sends these offerings, in hope to win
A cure to cleave and sunder sin from doom.

ORESTES: Earth and my father's grave, to you I call—
Give this her dream fulfilment, and thro' me.
I read it in each part coincident,
With what shall be; for mark, that serpent sprang
From the same womb as I, in swaddling bands
By the same hands was swathed, lipped the same breast,
And sucking forth the same sweet mother's-milk
Infused a clot of blood; and in alarm
She cried upon her wound the cry of pain.
The rede is clear: the thing of dread she nursed,
The death of blood she dies; and I, 'tis I,

In semblance of a serpent, that must slay her.
Thou art my seer, and thus I read the dream.

CHORUS: So do; yet ere thou doest, speak to us,
Siding some act, some, by not acting, aid.

ORESTES: Brief my command: I bid my sister pass
In silence to the house, and all I bid
This my design with wariness conceal,
That they who did by craft a chieftain slay
May by like craft and in like noose be ta'en
Dying the death which Loxias foretold—
Apollo, king and prophet undisproved.
I with this warrior Pylades will come
In likeness of a stranger, full equipt
As travellers come, and at the palace gates
Will stand, as stranger yet in friendship's bond
Unto this house allied; and each of us
Will speak the tongue that round Parnassus sounds,
Feigning such speech as Phocian voices use.
And what if none of those that tend the gates
Shall welcome us with gladness, since the house
With ills divine is haunted? if this hap,
We at the gate will bide, till, passing by,
Some townsman make conjecture and proclaim,
How? is Aegisthus here, and knowingly
Keeps suppliants aloof, by bolt and bar?
Then shall I win my way; and if I cross
The threshold of the gate, the palace' guard,
And find him throned where once my father sat—
Or if he come anon, and face to face
Confronting, drop his eyes from mine—I swear
He shall not utter, *Who art thou and whence?*
Ere my steel leap, and compassed round with death
Low he shall lie: and thus, full-fed with doom,
The Fury of the house shall drain once more
A deep third draught of rich unmingled blood.
But thou, O sister, look that all within
Be well prepared to give these things event.
And ye—I say 'twere well to bear a tongue
Full of fair silence and of fitting speech

As each beseems the time; and last, do thou,
Hermes the warder-god, keep watch and ward,
And guide to victory my striving sword.

(*Exit with Pylades*)

CHORUS: Many and marvellous the things of fear
      Earth's breast doth bear;
   And the sea's lap with many monsters teems,
   And windy levin-bolts and meteor gleams
      Breed many deadly things—
Unknown and flying forms, with fear upon their wings,
      And in their tread is death;
   And rushing whirlwinds, of whose blasting breath
     Man's tongue can tell.
     But who can tell aright the fiercer thing,
     The aweless soul, within man's breast inhabiting?
     Who tell, how, passion-fraught and love-distraught
     The woman's eager, craving thought
     Doth wed mankind to woe and ruin fell?
     Yea, how the loveless love that doth possess
     The woman, even as the lioness,
     Doth rend and wrest apart, with eager strife,
      The link of wedded life?

Let him be the witness, whose thought is not borne on light wings
   thro' the air,
But abideth with knowledge, what thing was wrought by Althea's
   despair;
For she marr'd the life-grace of her son, with ill counsel rekindled
   the flame
That was quenched as it glowed on the brand, what time from his
   mother he came,
With the cry of a new-born child; and the brand from the burning
   she won,
For the Fates had foretold it coeval, in life and in death, with her
   son.

Yea, and man's hate tells of another, even Scylla of murderous guile,
Who slew for an enemy's sake her father, won o'er by the wile
And the gifts of Cretan Minos, the gauds of the high-wrought gold;

For she clipped from her father's head the lock that should never
  wax old,
As he breathed in the silence of sleep, and knew not her craft and
  her crime—
But Hermes, the guard of the dead, doth grasp her, in fulness of time.

And since of the crimes of the cruel I tell, let my singing record
The bitter wedlock and loveless, the curse on these halls outpoured,
The crafty device of a woman, whereby did a chieftain fall,
A warrior stern in his wrath; the fear of his enemies all,—
A song of dishonour, untimely! and cold is the hearth that was warm
And ruled by the cowardly spear, the woman's unwomanly arm.

But the summit and crown of all crimes is that which in Lemnos
  befell;
A woe and a mourning it is, a shame and a spitting to tell;
And he that in after time doth speak of his deadliest thought,
Doth say, *It is like to the deed that of old time in Lemnos was wrought*;
And loathed of men were the doers, and perished, they and their
  seed,
For the gods brought hate upon them; none loveth the impious deed.

It is well of these tales to tell; for the sword in the grasp of Right
With a cleaving, a piercing blow to the innermost heart doth smite,
And the deed unlawfully done is not trodden down nor forgot,
When the sinner out-steppeth the law and heedeth the high God not;
But Justice hath planted the anvil, and Destiny forgeth the sword
That shall smite in her chosen time; by her is the child restored;
And, darkly devising, the Fiend of the house, world-cursed, will repay
The price of the blood of the slain that was shed in the bygone day.
(*Enter Orestes and Pylades, in guise of travellers*)
ORESTES: (*knocking at the palace gate*)
    What ho! slave, ho! I smite the palace gate
    In vain, it seems; what ho, attend within,—
    Once more, attend; come forth and ope the halls,
    If yet Aegisthus holds them hospitable.
SLAVE: (*from within*) Anon, anon!
(*Opens the door*)
    Speak, from what land art thou, and sent from whom?

ORESTES: Go, tell to them who rule the palace-halls,
    Since 'tis to them I come with tidings new—
    (Delay not—Night's dark car is speeding on,
    And time is now for wayfarers to cast
    Anchor in haven, wheresoe'er a house
    Doth welcome strangers)—that there now come forth
    Some one who holds authority within—
    The queen, or, if some man, more seemly were it;
    For when man standeth face to face with man,
    No stammering modesty confounds their speech,
    But each to each doth tell his meaning clear.
(*Enter Clytemnestra*)
CLYTEMNESTRA: Speak on, O strangers; have ye need
    of aught?
    Here is whate'er beseems a house like this—
    Warm bath and bed, tired Nature's soft restorer,
    And courteous eyes to greet you; and if aught
    Of graver import needeth act as well,
    That, as man's charge, I to a man will tell.
ORESTES: A Daulian man am I, from Phocis bound,
    And as with mine own travel-scrip self-laden
    I went toward Argos, parting hitherward
    With travelling foot, there did encounter me
    One whom I knew not and who knew not me,
    But asked my purposed way nor hid his own,
    And, as we talked together, told his name—
    Strophius of Phocis; then he said, "Good sir,
    Since in all case thou art to Argos bound,
    Forget not this my message, heed it well,
    Tell to his own, *Orestes is no more*.
    And—whatsoe'er his kinsfolk shall resolve,
    Whether to bear his dust unto his home,
    Or lay him here, in death as erst in life
    Exiled for aye, a child of banishment—
    Bring me their hest, upon thy backward road;
    For now in brazen compass of an urn
    His ashes lie, their dues of weeping paid."
    So much I heard, and so much tell to thee,
    Not knowing if I speak unto his kin

Who rule his home; but well, I deem, it were,
Such news should earliest reach a parent's ear.

CLYTEMNESTRA: Ah woe is me! thy word our ruin tells;
From roof-tree unto base are we despoiled.—
O thou whom nevermore we wrestle down,
Thou Fury of this home, how oft and oft
Thou dost descry what far aloof is laid,
Yea, from afar dost bend th' unerring bow
And rendest from my wretchedness its friends;
As now Orestes—who, a brief while since,
Safe from the mire of death stood warily,—
Was the home's hope to cure th' exulting wrong;
Now thou ordainest, *Let the ill abide*.

ORESTES: To host and hostess thus with fortune blest,
Lief had I come with better news to bear
Unto your greeting and acquaintanceship;
For what goodwill lies deeper than the bond
Of guest and host? and wrong abhorred it were,
As well I deem, if I, who pledged my faith
To one, and greetings from the other had,
Bore not aright the tidings 'twixt the twain.

CLYTEMNESTRA: Whate'er thy news, thou shalt not welcome lack,
Meet and deserved, nor scant our grace shall be.
Hadst them thyself not come, such tale to tell,
Another, sure, had borne it to our ears.
But lo! the hour is here when travelling guests,
Fresh from the daylong labour of the road,
Should win their rightful due. Take him within

(*To the slave*)

To the man-chamber's hospitable rest—
Him and these fellow-farers at his side;
Give them such guest-right as beseems our halls;
I bid thee do as thou shalt answer for it.
And I unto the prince who rules our home
Will tell the tale, and, since we lack not friends,
With them will counsel how this hap to bear

(*Exit Clytemnestra*)

CHORUS: So be it done—
Sister-servants, when draws nigh

Time for us aloud to cry
Orestes and his victory?

O holy earth and holy tomb
Over the grave-pit heaped on high,
Where low doth Agamemnon lie,
    The king of ships, the army's lord!
Now is the hour—give ear and come,
    For now doth Craft her aid afford,
And Hermes, guard of shades in hell,
Stands o'er their strife, to sentinel
    The dooming of the sword.
I wot the stranger worketh woe within—
For lo! I see come forth, suffused with tears,
Orestes' nurse. What ho, Kilissa—thou
Beyond the doors? Where goest thou? Methinks
Some grief unbidden walketh at thy side.

(*Enter Kilissa, a nurse*)

KILISSA: My mistress bids me, with what speed I may,
    Call in Aegisthus to the stranger guests,
    That he may come, and standing face to face,
    A man with men, may thus more clearly learn
    This rumour new. Thus speaking, to her slaves
    She hid beneath the glance of fictive grief
    Laughter for what is wrought—to her desire
    Too well; but ill, ill, ill besets the house,
    Brought by the tale these guests have told so clear.
    And he, God wot, will gladden all his heart
    Hearing this rumour. Woe and well-a-day!
    The bitter mingled cup of ancient woes,
    Hard to be borne, that here in Atreus' house
    Befel, was grievous to mine inmost heart,
    But never yet did I endure such pain.
    All else I bore with set soul patiently;
    But now—alack, alack!—Orestes dear,
    The day and night-long travail of my soul!
    Whom from his mother's womb, a new-born child,
    I clasped and cherished! Many a time and oft
    Toilsome and profitless my service was,

When his shrill outcry called me from my couch!
For the young child, before the sense is born,
Hath but a dumb thing's life, must needs be nursed
As its own nature bids. The swaddled thing
Hath nought of speech, whate'er discomfort come—
Hunger or thirst or lower weakling need,—
For the babe's stomach works its own relief.
Which knowing well before, yet oft surprised,
'Twas mine to cleanse the swaddling clothes—poor I
Was nurse to tend and fuller to make white;
Two works in one, two handicrafts I took,
When in mine arms the father laid the boy.
And now he's dead—alack and well-a-day!
Yet must I go to him whose wrongful power
Pollutes this house—fair tidings these to him!

CHORUS: Say then, with what array she bids him come?
KILISSA: What say'st thou! Speak more clearly for mine ear.
CHORUS: Bids she bring henchmen, or to come alone?
KLLISSA: She bids him bring a spear-armed body-guard.
CHORUS: Nay, tell not that unto our loathèd lord,
 But speed to him, put on the mien of joy,
 Say, *Come along, fear nought, the news is good:*
 A bearer can tell straight a twisted tale.
KILISSA: Does then thy mind in this new tale find joy?
CHORUS: What if Zeus bid our ill wind veer to fair?
KILISSA: And how? the home's hope with Orestes dies.
CHORUS: Not yet—a seer, though feeble, this might see.
KILISSA: What say'st thou? Know'st thou aught, this tale belying?
CHORUS: Go, tell the news to him, perform thine hest,—
 What the gods will, themselves can well provide.
KILISSA: Well, I will go, herein obeying thee;
 And luck fall fair, with favour sent from heaven.
(*Exit*)
CHORUS: Zeus, sire of them who on Olympus dwell,
  Hear thou, O hear my prayer!
 Grant to my rightful lords to prosper well
  Even as their zeal is fair!
 For right, for right goes up aloud my cry—
  Zeus, aid him, stand anigh!

Into his father's hall he goes
To smite his father's foes.
Bid him prevail! by thee on throne of triumph set,
Twice, yea and thrice with joy shall he acquit the debt.

Bethink thee, the young steed, the orphan foal
Of sire beloved by thee, unto the car
Of doom is harnessed fast.
Guide him aright, plant firm a lasting goal,
Speed thou his pace,—O that no chance may mar
The homeward course, the last!

And ye who dwell within the inner chamber
Where shines the storèd joy of gold—
Gods of one heart, O hear ye, and remember;
Up and avenge the blood shed forth of old,
With sudden rightful blow;
Then let the old curse die, nor be renewed
With progeny of blood,—
Once more, and not again, be latter guilt laid low!

O thou who dwell'st in Delphi's mighty cave,
Grant us to see this home once more restored
Unto its rightful lord!
Let it look forth, from veils of death, with joyous eye
Unto the dawning light of liberty;
And Hermes, Maia's child, lend hand to save,
Willing the right, and guide
Our state with Fortune's breeze adown the favouring tide.
Whate'er in darkness hidden lies,
He utters at his will;
He at his will throws darkness on our eye
By night and eke by day inscrutable.

Then, then shall wealth atone
The ills that here were done.
Then, then will we unbind,
Fling free on wafting wind
Of joy, the woman's voice that waileth now

In piercing accents for a chief laid low;
    And this our song shall be—
    Hail to the commonwealth restored!
    Hail to the freedom won to me!
All hail! for doom hath passed from him, my well-loved lord!

And thou, O child, when Time and Chance agree,
Up to the deed that for thy sire is done!
And if she wail unto thee, *Spare, O son*—
Cry, *Aid, O father*—and achieve the deed,
The horror of man's tongue, the gods' great need!
Hold in thy breast such heart as Perseus had,
The bitter woe work forth,
Appease the summons of the dead,
The wrath of friends on earth;
Yea, set within a sign of blood and doom,
And do to utter death him that pollutes thy home.

(*Enter Aegisthus*)

AEGISTHUS: Hither and not unsummoned have I come;
    For a new rumour, borne by stranger men
    Arriving hither, hath attained mine ears,
    Of hap unwished-for, even Orestes' death.
    This were new sorrow, a blood-bolter'd load
    Laid on the house that doth already bow
    Beneath a former wound that festers deep.
    Dare I opine these words have truth and life?
    Or are they tales, of woman's terror born,
    That fly in the void air, and die disproved?
    Canst thou tell aught, and prove it to my soul?

CHORUS: What we have heard, we heard; go thou within
    Thyself to ask the strangers of their tale.
    Strengthless are tidings, thro' another heard;
    Question is his, to whom the tale is brought.

AEGISTHUS: I too will meet and test the messenger,
    Whether himself stood witness of the death,
    Or tells it merely from dim rumour learnt:
    None shall cheat me, whose soul hath watchful eyes.

(*Exit*)

CHORUS: Zeus, Zeus! what word to me is given?

What cry or prayer, invoking heaven,
Shall first by me be utterèd?
What speech of craft? nor all revealing,
Nor all too warily concealing—
Ending my speech, shall aid the deed?
For lo! in readiness is laid
The dark emprise, the rending blade;
Blood-dropping daggers shall achieve
The dateless doom of Atreus' name,
Or—kindling torch and joyful flame
In sign of new-won liberty—
Once more Orestes shall retrieve
His father's wealth, and, throned on high,
Shall hold the city's fealty.
So mighty is the grasp whereby,
Heaven-holpen, he shall trip and throw,
Unseconded, a double foe
Ho for the victory!

(*A loud cry within*)

VOICE OF AEGISTHUS: Help, help, alas!
CHORUS: Ho there, ho! how is't within?
　　Is't done? is't over? Stand we here aloof
　　While it is wrought, that guiltless we may seem
　　Of this dark deed; with death is strife fulfilled.

(*Enter a slave*

SLAVE: O woe, O woe, my lord is done to death!
　　Woe, woe, and woe again, Ægisthus gone!
　　Hasten, fling wide the doors, unloose the bolts
　　Of the queen's chamber. O for some young strength
　　To match the need! but aid availeth nought
　　To him laid low for ever. Help, help, help!
　　Sure to deaf ears I shout, and call in vain
　　To slumber ineffectual. What ho!
　　The queen! how fareth Clytemnestra's self?
　　Her neck too, hers, is close upon the steel,
　　And soon shall sink, hewn thro' as justice wills.

(*Enter Clytemnestra*)

CLYTEMNESTRA: What ails thee, raising this ado for us?
SLAVE: I say the dead are come to slay the living.

CLYTEMNESTRA: Alack, I read thy riddles all too clear—
    We slew by craft and by like craft shall die.
    Swift, bring the axe that slew my lord of old;
    I'll know anon or death or victory—
    So stands the curse, so I confront it here.
(*Enter Orestes, his sword dropping with blood*)
ORESTES: Thee too I seek: for him what's done will serve.
CLYTEMNESTRA: Woe, woe! Aegisthus, spouse and champion,
    slain!
ORESTES: What lov'st the man? then in his grave lie down,
    Be his in death, desert him nevermore!
CLYTEMNESTSA Stay, child, and fear to strike. O son, this breast
    Pillowed thine head full oft, while, drowsed with sleep,
    Thy toothless mouth drew mother's milk from me.
ORESTES: Can I my mother spare? speak, Pylades,
PYLADES: Where then would fall the hest Apollo gave
    At Delphi, where the solemn compact sworn?
    Choose thou the hate of all men, not of gods.
ORESTES: Thou dost prevail; I hold thy counsel good.
(*To Clytemnestra*)
    Follow; I will slay thee at his side.
    With him whom in his life thou lovedst more
    Than Agamemnon, sleep in death, the meed
    For hate where love, and love where hate was due!
CLYTEMNESTRA: I nursed thee young; must I forego mine eld?
ORESTES: Thou slew'st my father; shalt thou dwell with me?
CLYTEMNESTRA: Fate bore a share in these things, O my child!
ORESTES: Fate also doth provide this doom for thee.
CLYTEMNESTRA: Beware, O my child, a parent's dying curse.
ORESTES: A parent who did cast me out to ill!
CLYTEMNESTRA: Not cast thee out, but to a friendly home.
ORESTES: Born free, I was by twofold bargain sold.
CLYTEMNESTRA: Where then the price that I received for
    thee?
ORESTES: The price of shame; I taunt thee not more plainly.
CLYTEMNESTRA: Nay, but recount thy father's lewdness too.
ORESTES: Home-keeping, chide not him who toils without.
CLYTEMNESTRA: 'Tis hard for wives to live as widows, child.
ORESTES: The absent husband toils for them at home.

CLYTEMNESTRA: Thou growest fain to slay thy mother, child
ORESTES: Nay, 'tis thyself wilt slay thyself, not I.
CLYTEMNESTRA: Beware thy mother's vengeful hounds from hell.
ORESTES: How shall I 'scape my father's, sparing thee?
CLYTEMNESTRA: Living, I cry as to a tomb, unheard.
ORESTES: My father's fate ordains this doom for thee.
CLYTEMNESTRA: Ah, me! this snake it was I bore and nursed.
ORESTES: Ay, right prophetic was thy visioned fear.
    Shameful thy deed was—die the death of shame!
(*Exit, driving Clytemnestra before him*)
CHORUS: Lo, even for these I mourn, a double death:
    Yet since Orestes, driven on by doom,
    Thus crowns the height of murders manifold,
    I say, 'tis well—that not in night and death
    Should sink the eye and light of this our home.

There came on Priam's race and name
    A vengeance; though it tarried long,
        With heavy doom it came.
Came, too, on Agamemnon's hall
        A lion-pair, twin swordsmen strong.
And last, the heritage doth fall
    To him, to whom from Pythian cave
    The god his deepest counsel gave.
Cry out, rejoice! our kingly hall
    Hath 'scaped from ruin—ne'er again
Its ancient wealth be wasted all
        By two usurpers, sin-defiled—
        An evil path of woe and bane!
On him who dealt the dastard blow
        Comes Craft, Revenge's scheming child.
And hand in hand with him doth go,
        Eager for fight,
The child of Zeus, whom men below
    Call Justice, naming her aright.
        And on her foes her breath
        Is as the blast of death;
For her the god who dwells in deep recess
        Beneath Parnassus' brow,

Summons with loud acclaim
To rise, though late and lame,
And come with craft that worketh righteousness.

For even o'er Powers divine this law is strong—
Thou shalt not serve the wrong.
To that which ruleth heaven beseems it that we bow.
Lo, freedom's light hath come!
Lo, now is rent away
The grim and curbing bit that held us dumb.
Up to the light, ye halls! this many a day
Too low on earth ye lay.
And Time, the great Accomplisher,
Shall cross the threshold, whensoe'er
He choose with purging hand to cleanse
The palace, driving all pollution thence.
And fair the cast of Fortune's die
Before our state's new lords shall lie,
Not as of old, but bringing fairer doom
Lo, freedom's light hath come!

(*The scene opens, disclosing Orestes standing over the corpses of Aegisthus and Clytemnestra; in one hand he holds his sword, in the other the robe in which Agamemnon was entangled and slain*)

ORESTES: There lies our country's twofold tyranny,
My father's slayers, spoilers of my home.
Erst were they royal, sitting on the throne,
And loving are they yet,—their common fate
Tells the tale truly, shows their trothplight firm.
They swore to work mine ill-starred father's death,
They swore to die together; 'tis fulfilled.
O ye who stand, this great doom's witnesses,
Behold this too, the dark device which bound
My sire unhappy to his death,—behold
The mesh which trapped his hands, enwound his feet!
Stand round, unfold it—'tis the trammel-net
That wrapped a chieftain; holds it that he see,
The father—not my sire, but he whose eye
Is judge of all things, the all-seeing Sun!
Let him behold my mother's damnèd deed,

Then let him stand, when need shall be to me,
Witness that justly I have sought and slain
My mother; blameless was Aegisthus' doom—
He died the death law bids adulterers die.
But she who plotted this accursèd thing
To slay her lord, by whom she bare beneath
Her girdle once the burden of her babes,
Beloved erewhile, now turned to hateful foes—
What deem ye of her? or what venomed thing,
Sea-snake or adder, had more power than she
To poison with a touch the flesh unscarred?
So great her daring, such her impious will.
How name her, if I may not speak a curse?
A lion-springe! a laver's swathing cloth,
Wrapping a dead man, twining round his feet—
A net, a trammel, an entangling robe?
Such were the weapon of some strangling thief,
The terror of the road, a cut-purse hound—
With such device full many might he kill,
Full oft exult in heat of villainy.
Ne'er have my house so cursed an indweller—
Heaven send me, rather, childless to be slain!
CHORUS: Woe for each desperate deed!
    Woe for the queen, with shame of life bereft!
    And ah, for him who still is left,
    Madness, dark blossom of a bloody seed!
ORESTES: Did she the deed or not? this robe gives proof,
    Imbrued with blood that bathed Aegisthus' sword:
    Look, how the spurted stain combines with time
    To blur the many dyes that once adorned
    Its pattern manifold! I now stand here,
    Made glad, made sad with blood, exulting, wailing—
    Hear, O thou woven web that slew my sire!
    I grieve for deed and death and all my home—
    Victor, pollution's damnèd stain for prize.
CHORUS: Alas, that none of mortal men
    Can pass his life untouched by pain!
    Behold, one woe is here—
    Another loometh near.

ORESTES: Hark ye and learn—for what the end
  shall be
  For me I know not: breaking from the curb
  My spirit whirls me off, a conquered prey,
  Borne as a charioteer by steeds distraught
  Far from the course, and madness in my breast
  Burneth to chant its song, and leap, and rave—
  Hark ye and learn, friends, ere my reason goes!
  I say that rightfully I slew my mother,
  A thing God-scorned, that foully slew my sire
  And chiefest wizard of the spell that bound me
  Unto this deed I name the Pythian seer
  Apollo, who foretold that if I slew,
  The guilt of murder done should pass from me;
  But if I spared, the fate that should be mine
  I dare not blazon forth—the bow of speech
  Can reach not to the mark, that doom to tell.
  And now behold me, how with branch and crown
  I pass, a suppliant made meet to go
  Unto Earth's midmost shrine, the holy ground
  Of Loxias, and that renownèd light
  Of ever-burning fire, to 'scape the doom
  Of kindred murder: to no other shrine
  (So Loxias bade) may I for refuge turn.
  Bear witness, Argives, in the after time,
  How came on me this dread fatality.
  Living, I pass a banished wanderer hence,
  To leave in death the memory of this cry.
CHORUS: Nay, but the deed is well; link not thy lips
  To speech ill-starred, nor vent ill-boding words—
  Who hast to Argos her full freedom given,
  Lopping two serpents' heads with timely blow.
ORESTES: Look, look, alas!
  Handmaidens, see—what Gorgon shapes throng up;
  Dusky their robes and all their hair enwound—
  Snakes coiled with snakes—off, off, I must away!
CHORUS: Most loyal of all sons unto thy sire,
  What visions thus distract thee? Hold, abide;
  Great was thy victory, and shalt thou fear?

ORESTES: These are no dreams, void shapes of haunting ill,
  But clear to sight my mother's hell-hounds come!
CHORUS: Nay, the fresh bloodshed still imbrues thine hands,
  And thence distraction sinks into thy soul.
ORESTES: O king Apollo—see, they swarm and throng—
  Black blood of hatred dripping from their eyes!
CHORUS: One remedy thou hast; go, touch the shrine
  Of Loxias, and rid thee of these woes.
ORESTES: Ye can behold them not, but I behold them.
  Up and away! I dare abide no more.
(*Exit*)
CHORUS: Farewell then as thou mayst,—the god thy friend
  Guard thee and aid with chances favouring.

  Behold, the storm of woe divine
  That the raves and beats on Atreus' line
    Its great third blast hath blown.
  First was Thyestes' loathly woe—
  The rueful feast of long ago,
    On children's flesh, unknown.
  And next the kingly chief's despite,
  When he who led the Greeks to fight
    Was in the bath hewn down.
  And now the offspring of the race
  Stands in the third, the saviour's place,
    To save—or to consume?
  O whither, ere it be fulfilled,
  Ere its fierce blast be hushed and stilled,
    Shall blow the wind of doom?
(*Exeunt*)

A Note About the Author

Aeschylus (c. 525–455 B.C.) was an ancient Greek playwright and soldier. Scholars' knowledge of the tragedy genre begins with Aeschylus' work, and because of this, he is dubbed the "father of tragedy." Aeschylus claimed his inspiration to become a writer stemmed from a dream he had in which the god Dionysus encouraged him to write a play. While it is estimated that he wrote just under one hundred plays, only seven of Aeschylus' work was able to be recovered.

A Note from the Publisher

Spanning many genres, from non-fiction essays to literature classics to children's books and lyric poetry, Mint Edition books showcase the master works of our time in a modern new package. The text is freshly typeset, is clean and easy to read, and features a new note about the author in each volume. Many books also include exclusive new introductory material. Every book boasts a striking new cover, which makes it as appropriate for collecting as it is for gift giving. Mint Edition books are only printed when a reader orders them, so natural resources are not wasted. We're proud that our books are never manufactured in excess and exist only in the exact quantity they need to be read and enjoyed.

Discover more of your favorite classics with Bookfinity™.

- Track your reading with custom book lists.
- Get great book recommendations for your personalized Reader Type.
- Add reviews for your favorite books.
- AND MUCH MORE!

Visit **bookfinity.com** and take the fun Reader Type quiz to get started.

Enjoy our classic and modern companion pairings!

Bookfinity is a registered trademark of Ingram Book Group LLC. © 2023 Bookfinity. All rights reserved.

www.ingramcontent.com/pod-product-compliance
Lightning Source LLC
Chambersburg PA
CBHW020608130626
46552CB00007B/3102